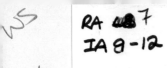

Grow up, Dad!

by

Narinder Dhami

Illustrated by

You do not need to read this page –
just get on with the book!

First published in 2005 in Great Britain by
Barrington Stoke Ltd, Sandeman House, Trunk's Close,
55 High Street, Edinburgh EH1 1SR
www.barringtonstoke.co.uk

This edition based on *Grow Up, Dad!*, published by
Barrington Stoke in 2004

ISBN 1-842993-23-2

Printed in Great Britain by Bell & Bain Ltd

Meet The Author – Narinder Dhami

What is your favourite animal?
Cats – I have five of them
What is your favourite boy's name?
Freddie
What is your favourite girl's name?
Natasha
What is your favourite food?
Curry, especially my mum's
What is your favourite music?
1970s' punk and bhangra
What is your favourite hobby?
Watching football (I support Wolves)

Meet The Illustrator – Mike Phillips

What is your favourite animal?
Dog
What is your favourite boy's name?
Ben (my son's name)
What is your favourite girl's name?
Hannah and Olivia (my daughters)
What is your favourite food?
Cheese
What is your favourite music?
Anything that makes my feet tap
What is your favourite hobby?
Armchair cricket supporting

For Robert

Contents

Chapter 1
A Fool!

Do you know what I am?

I'm a fool!

That's right.

A fool. A mug. A loser.

I'm all of those things.

You see I could be sitting in the sun in Florida with my mum.

But I'm not.

I'm here in my bedroom, and Dad's yelling at me like he always does.

"Robbie! Have you sorted your bedroom yet? ROBBIE!" Dad was yelling up at me and he was mad, I could tell. So what? Dad was always mad at me these days.

I pressed the button on my computer. The screen lit up.

Have you ever felt really fed up with your family? Have you ever wanted to get rid of them, and start again with a new lot? I felt like that about my dad. I wish there was a Dad Swap Shop. I'd take him down there and get a new one.

Dad was looking for a fight with me.
I could hear him running up the stairs. Now
he was at the top. *BANG!*

My bedroom door crashed open.

"Robbie, do you hear what I'm saying?"
Dad yelled. He was very angry. "Have you
sorted your bedroom yet?"

I didn't say a thing. I didn't have to.
I hadn't made my bed, my school uniform
was on the floor and there were CDs
everywhere. So now Dad and I were going
to have a big fight. We were always
fighting.

"You *haven't* sorted anything!" Dad
yelled. "How many times do I have to tell
you?"

"I'll do it later," I said, and I kept on
looking at my computer screen. I wanted to

check my e-mails and see if Mum had replied to my last message.

"That's what you always say," Dad said. He rushed into the room and fell over my sports bag. I tried not to smile.

"You spend too much time on that computer," Dad snapped. "Get this room sorted, Robbie. Now."

"Later." I swung round in my chair and looked angrily at Dad.

"*Now*," Dad said.

One of us would have to give in, and it wasn't going to be me.

Just then the doorbell rang. I slid out of my chair, and ran down to see who it was.

Saved by the bell, I thought.

Dad's been like this ever since Mum left. He used to be fun, but now he's a pain. He's hardly ever at home because he's always doing overtime at work. We never do stuff together any more. He nags me all the time. *Robbie, sort your bedroom. Robbie, do your homework. Robbie, do this. Robbie, do that.*

I wish I'd gone to America with Mum and her new boyfriend.

When Mum and Dad split up, they said it was up to me where I wanted to live. I could go to Florida with Mum and Scott, or stay here with Dad.

Now you know why I'm a fool.

I said I'd stay with Dad. I didn't like to think of him all alone, and I knew he didn't want me to go. Big mistake. All Dad wanted was someone to yell at. And I'm getting sick of it.

I opened the front door. My best mate Joe stood outside.

****

Let's go back a bit.

Joe *used* to be my best mate, but right now I don't want to hang out with him any more.

"Hi, Robbie," Joe said. He looked down at his feet. "Um – me and some of the lads are going to the park to play footy."

Joe and I have had a lot of fights this week. We had a big one at school yesterday. Joe said I looked at things the wrong way. Just because I was moaning about Dad. And you know what else Joe said? He said I should give Dad a break!

Yeah, right. When was Dad going to give *me* a break? I missed Mum, and I was tired of being nagged all the time.

Joe and I stood there, looking at each other.

"Well?" Joe said at last. "Do you want to come or not?"

I wanted to say "Yes". But I didn't.

"No, thanks," I said.

Joe looked upset. "I suppose you're going out with your *new* mates," he said.

I frowned. "What new mates?"

"Crusher Capstick and his gang," said Joe. "I saw you hanging around with them after school yesterday."

Crusher Capstick was in our class at school. He was a pain and a bully and a pest, and all the teachers hated him. Most of the kids did, too. Crusher was always starting fights or talking back at the teachers or bunking off school. But he was a laugh, and he didn't care about anything or anyone. I wanted to be like him.

"Leave me alone," I said, and slammed the door in Joe's face.

Nice one, Robbie! Now my dad *and* my best friend hated me.

My life was a mess.

And it could only get worse.

What should I do, stay here with Dad, or go to Florida? I didn't know any more.

I sat down and thought for a bit. Then I made up my mind. I'd e-mail Mum and ask her to send me a ticket to America. I'd move in with her and Scott, and everything would be cool.

I didn't care if I never saw Dad again. Or Joe.

Dad wasn't going to miss me anyway. He was at work most of the time. And if he wanted to nag someone, he could get a dog!

I ran upstairs. I'd e-mail my mum right now, and by next week, I'd be gone. I felt a pain deep down inside me, but I knew it was for the best.

Dad had gone into his bedroom and shut the door. I was glad. I didn't want to tell him I was leaving until it was all sorted out.

I sat down and clicked on my e-mails.

I hope Mum lets me bring the computer, I thought. My computer was the best friend I had right now. I wasn't going to leave it behind.

I only had one new e-mail, and it wasn't from Mum. It was junk mail. But for once, it looked interesting.

Is your life a mess?

Do you think it can only get worse?

WE CAN HELP!

Chapter 2
Kaboom!

I never open junk mail. Dad always tells me to delete it, in case it's got a virus.

But this time I didn't press delete. I sat and looked at the message on my screen.

Is your life a mess?

Do you think it can only get worse?

They were the same words I'd said to myself just now. How odd.

WE CAN HELP!

I looked at the *Delete* key, but I didn't press it. Instead I clicked on the e-mail so I could read it all.

KABOOM!

I got a real shock. A shower of silver stars exploded out of the screen. They were so bright that they lit up the whole room. I blinked.

Is your life a mess?

The words fizzed around on the screen in front of me. They went so fast that I started to feel dizzy.

Do you think it can only get worse?

Pink and blue rockets shot all over the screen. Now I felt really dizzy. I was so dazzled by the bright colours that I could only just read the words.

We can help.

But be careful what you wish for.

You might just get it!

Someone tapped me on the arm.

"OH!" I spun round.

I hadn't heard Dad come into the room. I was so shocked, my finger slipped and the message vanished. It was better that way. I didn't want Dad to see that I'd been looking at junk mail.

Dad sounded cross. "Were you looking at junk mail?" he asked.

"No," I said.

"What have I told you?" Dad snapped. "You must always delete junk mail in case it's a virus—"

"I know," I cut in. "Will you stop nagging me?"

"I only nag because you don't do what you're told," Dad said. "Look at this mess." He waved his hand at the room. "I've asked you to sort your room a hundred times."

"I'll do it when I'm ready," I told him. "I've got other things to think about."

"Like what?" asked Dad.

He bent down and picked up my school shirt.

"You don't know how lucky you are, Robbie," he said, sitting on my bed. It was as if he was talking to himself. "I wish I was 11 years old like you, with no problems to sort out and nothing to worry about."

"Oh yeah?" I yelled.

I was very angry. Did Dad think my life was really that great?

"Well, I wish you were the same age as me," I yelled at him. "Then you'd see that I've got LOADS of problems!"

Be careful what you wish for.

You might just get it!

Chapter 3
All Change

There was no flash of silver light, no puff of smoke. I just felt a bit dizzy again. That was all.

But something had happened. Something *huge*.

Could this be true? I blinked. Once. Twice. Three times. It was true.

Dad was still sitting on my bed. He still had my school shirt in his hand. But he wasn't Dad.

He'd shrunk. He was smaller than I was. His shirt and tie were much too big for him. He looked like a kid dressing up in his dad's clothes. His hair was weird, too. He always wore it short, but now it was long and messy, just like mine.

I gasped.

Dad looked *11 years old*.

"What's happened to me?" Dad asked in a high voice. "I feel funny. I *sound* funny too!"

I gazed at him. I didn't know what to say.

"Look in the mirror," I said at last.

Dad stood up and went over to the mirror. He jumped back when he saw himself.

"Is this some kind of trick, Robbie?" he asked.

I might have known Dad would blame me for what had happened to him! Then I remembered the e-mail.

Be careful what you wish for.

You might just get it!

"Robbie!" Dad was starting to sound very upset. "Is this a joke?"

"No," I said. "You've shrunk. Look at your clothes. They're too big for you."

Dad stared down at himself. His eyes were popping out of his head.

"What's going on?" he asked.

"I think you're 11 years old," I told him.

Dad looked at me as if I was mad.

"You wanted to be 11," I said. "And now you are."

"Don't be silly," Dad began. Then he looked at himself this way and that in the mirror. He shut his eyes and opened them again.

"Oh no!" he said at last. "I *am* 11 years old!" He sat down on my bed and put his head in his hands. "I'm ill! There's something very wrong with me!"

"I don't think so," I said. How could opening the junk e-mail have done this? Wishes and magic spells were for kids.

But something odd had happened.

25

Dad jumped up from the bed and tripped over his long jeans.

"I'd better go to the doctor's," he said. He sounded upset.

"It's Saturday," I told him. "They're closed."

"We'll go to the hospital then." Dad still looked very shocked. "You'll have to lend me some of your clothes, Robbie. I can't go like this."

I gave Dad a pair of my jeans, a T-shirt and some trainers.

"I don't know why you're so upset," I said. "You wanted to be 11 years old again, didn't you?"

"Don't be cheeky, Robbie," he snapped. "I'm still your dad."

"But you're only 11!" I said with a grin. "And you're smaller than I am!"

Dad looked at me angrily, and rushed out of the room. I went after him. Before I left, I looked at my computer screen. Should I read that e-mail again? Would it help Dad get back to normal?

"Don't be stupid," I told myself. "You don't believe in magic!"

Dad was in the hall. He had the car keys in his hand.

"Dad!" I said with a grin. "You can't drive to the hospital!"

Dad looked cross. "Why not?" he asked.

"Because you're 11!" I was really laughing now.

"I only *look* 11," Dad replied. "Inside I'm still 32. And it's miles to the hospital. We're going by car."

"I don't think this is a good idea," I told him, as we went out.

Our silver car was parked at the side of the road. Dad walked over and unlocked it.

"Get in, Robbie," he said, and slid into the driver's seat.

I got in next to him. But I had to grin when I saw that Dad's feet didn't even reach the pedals!

Dad turned red. "I'll just move the seat forward," he said.

He was moving the seat when there was a tap at the window. We both looked up.

A policeman was looking in at us.

"I told you this wasn't a good idea," I said to Dad.

Dad opened the window, trying to look cool.

"Hello, officer," he said.

The policeman didn't look very happy. "And what are you two kids up to?" he asked. You could see he didn't trust us, not one bit.

"Well—" Dad began.

I gave him a nudge.

"Ow!" said Dad.

"Me and my brother are just getting something for my dad," I said rather fast. I pulled out a map from under the seat. "We're going back inside now."

"But—" Dad began again.

"Stop it," I said to him. "Or I'll tell our dad."

"That isn't funny, Robbie," Dad said softly, but he got out of the car all the same.

We went back to the house. The policeman stood and watched us the whole time. He only walked off when we'd gone inside and shut the door.

"Do you still think it's a good idea to take the car?" I asked.

"Maybe not," Dad said. He'd gone a bit red. "We'll walk into town and get the bus."

We set off again. It was really weird having a dad the same age as me. And Dad still kept on nagging me. "Robbie, do up your shoelaces. Robbie, mind that lady with

the baby buggy. Robbie, don't run across the road." It was awful getting told off by someone who was the same age as me!

We were walking down to catch the bus when Dad stopped.

"Oh no!" he gasped.

"What?"

"Look over there," Dad said. "It's my boss, Mr Green!"

Mr Green was coming our way.

"Quick!" Dad grabbed my arm. "We've got to hide. I can't let him see me like this!"

"Don't worry," I told Dad. "He won't know who you are."

"You may be right," Dad agreed, but he shook his head.

Mr Green had seen us, and was smiling at me. I'd met him a few times before. He seemed quite nice, but Dad said he was awful in the office. He told me it was Mr Green who made him do so much overtime.

"Hello, Robbie," called Mr Green. "Nice to see you again." He looked at Dad. "And who's this?"

"I'm one of his mates," said Dad.

"Well, nice to meet you," he said. "And how's your dad, Robbie?"

"He's not too bad," I replied. "He's just not feeling himself at the moment."

I thought that was quite funny, but Dad looked cross.

Mr Green nodded. "Yes, your dad's working too hard," he said. "I keep telling him to slow down, but he says he's fine."

My mouth fell open. That's not what Dad had said to *me*.

"Tell him from me to take it easy." Mr Green waved at us and went on his way.

I turned round and looked at Dad hard. He was bright red.

"What's going on, Dad?" I asked. "You said you *had* to spend all that time at the office."

"Well ..." Dad mumbled. "The thing is, I need the cash. We haven't got the money from your mum's job anymore. That's why I've been doing so much overtime."

For a moment I felt angry with myself. Of course we had less money now. But then I felt angry with Dad, too.

"Why didn't you tell me?" I asked him.

"Because it's up to me to sort it out," said Dad.

"You didn't have to lie to me. I'm not a kid!"

"Yes, you are," Dad said.

"Well, so are you!" I yelled. "So there!"

Chapter 4
Crusher

Dad looked really angry. I didn't know what he was going to do next. But then we heard a shout behind us.

"Robbie! Hey, Robbie!"

I looked round. Crusher Capstick and his gang were coming down the street. Crusher was out in front. He had his baseball cap on back to front, and he looked pretty cool.

"Hey, Crusher," I called back. "How's things?"

"Crusher?" Dad said. "What kind of a name is that?"

Crusher and the others stopped in front of us, and looked Dad up and down.

"Who's your geeky mate, Robbie?" Crusher asked with a grin. The rest of the gang, Ed, Rocky, Kirk and Dave, all laughed.

"This is my—" I stopped myself. I had almost said *Dad*. "This is Terry."

"Please call me Mr Carter," Dad said coldly to Crusher.

"Ooooh!" Crusher grinned. "Mr Carter, eh? Do you hear that, lads? Well, you can call me Mr Capstick!"

The others laughed. I didn't. I didn't like the way things were going.

"Crusher Capstick?" Dad said. "I know that name." He turned to me. "Robbie, is this the boy who's always in trouble at school? Is he a friend of yours?"

I was stuck. I didn't want Dad to know I'd been hanging around with Crusher's gang.

"Yeah, I am," said Crusher. He put his arm round me. "Robbie's in our gang. Aren't you, Rob?"

"Sort of," I said. I couldn't look at Dad.

"I think you and I had better have a little chat, Robbie," Dad said. "I don't want you getting into trouble, too."

Crusher and the others laughed even more.

"Listen to him!" Crusher said. "Who does he think he is? He sounds like your dad!"

"I don't want any cheek from you, thank you," Dad replied crossly.

Crusher stopped laughing and looked angry. Why couldn't Dad remember that he was 11 years old?

"Hey, Rob." Crusher slapped me on the back. "You don't want to hang around with this weirdo, do you? We're on our way to the old factory. Why don't you come with us?"

"Yeah, why don't you come with us?" said the others. I opened my mouth to say something. But Dad got in first.

"The old factory?" he said with a frown. "I don't let Robbie play there. It's much too dangerous."

Crusher looked at me with a glint in his eye. "Are you going to listen to this bossy little twit, or are you going to come with us?" he asked.

"Robbie's staying right here," Dad said loudly.

I made up my mind. "I'm coming," I said.

Chapter 5
Trouble

"Robbie, I said no!" Dad yelled after me as I walked off with Crusher and his gang. "Come back here!"

But there was nothing he could do. I mean, he was only 11! I kept on walking.

"Let's run for it," Crusher yelled. "Then we can leave that boring little geek behind."

We ran off down the street. When we got to the corner, I looked back. Dad was running after us, but he was a long way behind. He wasn't as fit as he used to be. He was panting.

I felt a bit bad. I knew I shouldn't have run off. But Dad was getting on my nerves with all that nagging. I was going to enjoy myself for a change.

"That's got rid of *him*!" Crusher laughed. By the time we got to the next corner, we'd left Dad far behind. "Come on, Robbie. The factory's just down here."

The tall old factory stood behind the High Street. It had lots of windows and doors which were all boarded up. It looked quite scary.

"How do we get in?" I asked.

Crusher winked at me. "Let's go round the back," he said.

One of the boards on a window at the back of the factory was loose. We pulled it to one side and got through the gap.

It was cold and damp inside. There was rubbish everywhere. It was almost dark inside and dead spooky. I didn't like it at all, but I tried not to show it.

"I wonder if that stupid mate of yours will follow us," Crusher said.

"He's not stupid," I said. Then I wished I'd said nothing as Crusher turned on me.

"OK." Crusher folded his arms. "I wonder if that *weird* mate of yours will follow us."

"He's not weird," I said. I didn't like hearing Crusher talk about my dad like that.

"You know what?" Crusher's voice was very calm, but it sent shivers up and down my spine. "You're starting to get on my nerves."

"Yeah," said Ed, Rocky, Kirk and Dave. "You're starting to get on our nerves too."

Crusher jabbed me in the chest with his finger. It hurt. "You're just as weird as your stupid mate," he went on. "So it's up to you to show us that you're not."

"How?" I asked, trying to look brave.

Crusher smiled. "Well," he said, "why don't you go up to the top floor? That will show us you're not a boring geek."

That sounded easy. Too easy. I looked around and saw that all the stairs were boarded up.

"I can't," I said. "There's no way up."

"Oh, yes, there is," Crusher replied with a grin. He pointed at a broken drainpipe in the corner of the factory. It went right up to the roof. The others grinned.

I looked at the drainpipe. I was sure it would snap if I tried to go up it. And when I got to the top floor, it might not be safe to walk around. I could have a really bad fall.

There was no way I was going up there.

"Go on." Crusher gave me a push. "All you've got to do is get up that drainpipe."

"Robbie! Don't do it!" called a voice I knew well.

Dad was coming in through the window. I groaned. Now things were going to get even more tricky.

"Robbie!" Dad rushed over to us. His face was red. "What do you think you're doing? I can't believe you'd be so stupid!"

"I wasn't going to—" I began.

"You're coming home with me right now," Dad went on. He didn't trust me. So what's new?

I'd never felt so cross in my life.

So I did something I'd wanted to do all day. I ran at Dad, and pushed him over onto the dusty floor.

Then I jumped on top of him, and we began to fight.

Chapter 6
The Fight

Crusher and his gang cheered.

"Fight! Fight!" they yelled, as Dad and I rolled across the factory floor.

We were both useless fighters. We pushed and pulled and tugged, but neither of us could get a punch in.

Then I saw the look on Dad's face.

What on earth was I *doing*?

I was fighting with my 11-year-old dad! This was crazy!

I let go of Dad and started to laugh. Dad blinked at me. Then he grinned and he began to laugh, too.

"What's so funny?" Crusher asked, looking puzzled. But we were both laughing too much to reply.

"I want to know what's going on!" Crusher said crossly. Dad and I didn't reply.

"Right, that's it!" Crusher yelled. "Unless you tell me what's going on, you're dead!"

"Now, you listen to me," Dad said, going up to Crusher. "It's about time you stopped being such a bully. I'm going to have a word with your parents, young man."

Crusher went purple.

"Dad, you're 11 years old," I said softly in his ear. "And there's only one way out of this."

"What's that?" asked Dad.

"RUN!" I yelled.

Chapter 7
Football Star

I ran off across the factory, dragging Dad with me.

"Get 'em!" Crusher shouted.

We dived out of the window and ran for it. Behind us we could hear Crusher and his gang yelling at each other as they all tried to get out of the window at the same time.

Dad and I dashed down the road. There was a rubbish skip on the corner. Dad grabbed my arm and pulled me behind it.

We stood there and waited. A moment later we heard footsteps.

"Come on!" Crusher shouted. "They can't be far away. That Robbie's dead when I get my hands on him!"

We heard them rush past us. Then there was silence.

Dad looked out from behind the skip. "They've gone," he said with a grin. "They didn't even think of looking behind the skip!"

I smiled back at him. "Crusher's a bit thick," I replied. Crusher *was* stupid. I don't know why I ever thought he was cool.

"Brains can beat a bully every time!" Dad told me with a smile.

"Yeah," I said, "until I go to school on Monday. Crusher's going to be waiting for me."

Dad frowned. "I forgot about that," he said. "Don't worry, Robbie. We'll sort something out."

"Thanks, Dad," I said. "Now, hadn't we better get to the hospital?"

"Yes, you're right," Dad agreed. "Let's go through the park."

We set off again. Dad and I were feeling better about each other now. It still wasn't like it used to be. But it was a start.

"I wasn't going to go up that drainpipe, you know," I told him.

Dad looked rather ashamed. "I know, son," he replied. "I was just worried, that's all. I do trust you."

"Thanks," I said.

A gang of boys were playing football in the park. It was Sam, Ben, Tom, Leroy and Darren, who were all in my class at school. My mate Joe was there, too.

"Hi," I said, feeling my face go red. Would Joe speak to me? After all, I'd been pretty horrible to him.

"Hey, Robbie," said Joe with a smile. He looked at Dad. "Who's this?"

"This is my mate, Terry," I said.

Joe frowned. "Have we met before?" he asked. "You look like someone I know."

Dad and I grinned at each other.

"Do you two want to play football with us?" Joe went on.

I thought Dad would say no. But he smiled and nodded.

"Well, maybe just for five minutes," he said. "Come on, Robbie."

We ran across the grass to join the others. Sam, Ben, Tom, Leroy and Darren looked really pleased to see us. I'd forgotten I had so many good mates.

We started playing. Dad and I were on the same team, and Dad was brilliant. He couldn't run very fast because he wasn't very fit, but he could do loads of tricks. He

slid the ball through Darren's legs, and passed to me. I hit the ball hard, and it flew past Ben. Goal!

"Your mate's fantastic!" said Joe, as he slapped me on the back. "I wish he came to our school. He could be in our team!"

I smiled. But then I saw Crusher Capstick and his gang marching towards us.

"Oi!" Crusher shouted angrily. "Come here, Robbie! You *and* that stupid mate of yours!"

I stayed where I was. Dad, Joe, Ben, Tom, Sam, Darren and Leroy came and stood next to me.

"What do you want, Crusher?" I asked.

"You're not in my gang any more, you wimp!" Crusher told me.

"Good," I said. "Anything else?"

Crusher made his hands into fists. But then he looked round at me and all my mates. He only had Ed, Rocky, Kirk and Dave to back him up.

"No," Crusher said. "Just keep out of my way from now on!"

"Don't worry," I replied. "I will."

We all laughed as Crusher and his gang ran off.

"I don't think you'll have any more trouble from him!" said Dad. "Now, what about this game?"

Dad scored two goals, and we won 3-1. Then we had to go.

"Bye, Joe," I called. "See you at school on Monday."

"OK." Joe waved at me. "Listen, my dad's joining a new football team at the sports centre. He told me to ask your dad to join, too."

I looked at Dad. "I'll tell him," I replied.

"Are you getting on better with him now?" Joe asked.

I laughed. "Yeah, much better!"

"You should join that football team," I told Dad as we walked off.

"I will," said Dad. "I'd forgotten how much I enjoyed playing." Then he added, "Look, Robbie, I know things haven't been easy since your mum left. But I'm going to try harder from now on."

"Me, too," I agreed. "I just wish we could get on this well when you go back to being Dad again!"

Chapter 8
Dad's Grown Up!

All at once I felt a bit dizzy. I blinked and shook my head.

Dad was standing in front of me. It *was* Dad! He was 32 years old again. He looked normal, except that his jeans and T-shirt were much too small for him!

"I'm all right again!" Dad gasped. "Thank goodness."

"Do you feel OK?" I asked.

Dad nodded. "I feel fine."

"You look as if you're going to burst out of those clothes!" I laughed. He was getting some very funny looks. "Come on, let's go home."

We hurried home. Dad went off to change and I turned my computer on. But that weird junk e-mail had vanished from the screen.

Dad came in as I turned my computer off. "I still don't understand what happened," he said. He looked puzzled. "Still, I'm back to normal now. That's all that matters." He grinned at me. "Shall we watch a video tonight, and order a pizza?"

"Great!" I grinned. "We haven't done that for ages."

"Things are going to be different now," Dad replied.

Just then the doorbell rang. It was Joe.

"Hi," he said. "You left your wallet at the park, Robbie." And he handed it over.

"Why don't you stay, Joe?" Dad said. "We're having a pizza."

"Great!" Joe said with a grin. "Where's your mate, Terry?"

I looked at Dad. "Oh, he's around somewhere," I replied. And we both started to laugh.

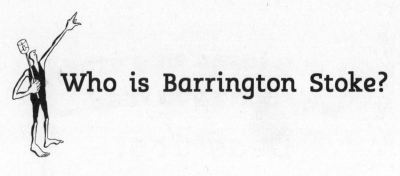

Who is Barrington Stoke?

Barrington Stoke went from place to place with his lamp in his hand. Everywhere he went, he told stories to children. Some were happy, some were sad, some were funny and some were scary.

The children always wanted more. When it got dark, they had to go home to bed. They went to look for Barrington Stoke the next day, but he had gone.

The children never forgot the stories. They told them to each other and to their children and their grandchildren. You see, good stories are magic and they can live for ever.